A Planetary Fairytale
Friendship

by Simonne Joy Murphy
Illustrations by Molly A Sullivan

A Planetary Fairytale
Friendship

by Simonne Joy Murphy

Cover and illustrations by Molly A Sullivan

International Standard Book Number
978-1-934976-61-6

Published by ACS Publications
an imprint of Starcrafts LLC
334-A Calef Highway, Epping, NH 03042

http://www.astrocom.com
http://www.acspublications.com
http://www.starcraftspublishing.com

This book is dedicated
to all my friends.
Thanks for
standing by me!
I love you

In our galaxy, the Milky Way, which is not so far away, the planets that circle around our bright Sun were busy looking out for each other, while also attending to their own jobs.

Neptune and Uranus were close enough in their orbits to talk with each other. Uranus was having a rough day, worrying about what the others thought of him after he had upset them in the past. "Oh my," he sighed, "I just hope that I've made things OK again."

Neptune replied, "Don't worry about the past so much! Just do your best now."

Uranus looked at Neptune with a grin, "Thank you! You're right. I'll try my best from now on to think first before I act. It is upsetting, though, to be so different and have to rotate around on my side instead of staying right side up like all the rest of you.

Neptune replied, 'I understand and you're right. It can be hard sometimes to feel different, but it is our differences that also make each of us special. I have faith in you!"

"Me too," said Venus. "I like that you are so unique, Uranus. Remember sometimes it is easier to do the popular thing instead of what you know is right for you. Believe in yourself!" Venus would hug Uranus and all the other planets if she could, since her main purpose among the planets is to spread love.

"Think about it, Uranus!" said Mercury, "There is no other planet just like you!"

Eris spoke up, "Of course, we are all different. Look at what happens when some of us take a little time to slow down. Then people who live on Earth get upset because they think we're suddenly moving backwards.

Earth said, "Well, you have no idea what it is like here, with all the people who live on me with all their different ideas. It just seems to them like everything changes too often and too fast!"

Moon and Ceres spoke up, "We care about you, Uranus. We see that you're trying to do your best. We care about all of you.

Mars had been quietly watching until now, when he said, "Come on, my friends. I know I have the tendency of not worrying very much about what others are thinking about me. I know this sometimes gets me in trouble, but I'm just trying to take action and do the best job that I can.

Jupiter, who had been quietly listening to the others, now said, "As long as we are all truthful and do what we think is right, we should be happy. I know that is not always easy, but in the end, it works out for the best."

Jupiter never had a problem being heard, since as the largest planet, he's one big guy in the sky! But Eris spoke up in response, saying "I'm not sure I can totally agree with you, Jupiter. Not everyone can handle the truth— or deal with it. Maybe it's better to bend or break the rules sometimes. "

"I disagree," said the Sun. "We all have to be true to ourselves and to what each of us stand for, even if that is not always popular."

"Oh, I know what it is like to be unpopular!" said Eris, as she blushed. "How would any of you like it if you had been named after a mythological goddess of discord? Just because of that name, I haven't been anybody's favorite planet. It's just not fair! Venus is named for a goddess of love, Jupiter is a king, and Mercury is named for a god who can fly with wings on his feet. Why am I stuck with discord? It's just not at all fair!"

"You're right! It isn't fair, said the Sun, "but we all need to learn to work with our challenges."

Out of this world book of
Art & Crafts
Im ok Your ok
Book of Dragons
I Think Therefore I Am
Black Holes
The UNIVERSE
Cats
Good Aliens/Bad Aliens
The Milky Way Galaxy
Believe in Me

The spines of the books read, from left to right:

- Good Communication Skills
- ARE YOU MY ALIEN
- How to get along well with others
- Why we love Pluto
- Space
- To be a Good Listener
- Friendship
- Retrograde

"Yes!" Mercury said, "Look at me!" How am I supposed to be able to read all of these books when I don't have any arms? Do you all realize how much we can learn from books? It is amazing!

The others smiled at little Mercury. Sometimes he had funny ideas.

"I like things to be in order," said Saturn, "but I know that sometimes there is a mess. So, I have to learn to accept that things can't always be exactly like I want them to be. We can all learn from each other."

"I like change!" said Pluto. "Change is good for us every so often, even when we don't see at that time. Besides, if things always stayed the same, how boring would that be?

"Look at me" said Moon. I change more often than any of you—every month! Did you know that the word month comes from me?   Think moon-th. The people who live on earth see me in different phases every month, and they time things by my changing shape.

The others had to chuckle at the Moon. She was so kind and beautiful. They all loved when she spread out her Moonbeams. Moon and all her splendor made them all happy—and the earthlings, too.

"Well, some of you are a bit slow and I like things done quickly. Sometimes I'm just impatient." said Mars

Saturn chimed in, "Maybe you ought to slow down just a bit and think about how you act affects others."

"Come on Saturn," said Mars. "Not all of us need to take as much time as you do! You are just way too slow!"

"But, I need to think things through before I act," said Saturn.

"Well, do you have to take SO long?" asked Mars.

"Well, I'm sorry I annoy you," said Saturn, "but now you've really hurt my feelings!"

"Oh, I'm sorry," Mars said. "There goes my temper again!" He looked around at all the others as he said, "Well, you all know I can have a bit of a temper. Does this make you not like me?"

NO!" said all of the other planets. "That's not it. We like you, but sometimes you're just not at all easy to be with, especially when that temper of yours shows. We all know that everything can't be happy all the time, and Mars, part of your job is to show us that it is okay to blow off some of our hidden feelings sometimes! You are still valuable to us as a friend."

This made Mars feel better.

Through all of this, Sun was very pleased with how his planets were behaving. You see, each and every planet is different and each offers something to the others that can help bring everything into order and harmony.

For this is Friendship.

About the Author—Simonne Murphy

Simonne Murphy is the one on the staff of Starcrafts LLC and Astro Computing Services who always knows where everything is and how to fix it, even when (or maybe especially when the principal (owner) is frustrated. Simonne is addicted to books (she was once a librarian) and is a primary editor and profreader for all we publish. *A Planetary Fairytale* is the second book she has written for us. The first one was *Ceres*, written just after asteroid Ceres was promoted to planet in 2006. But now that she's gotten off the ground as a writer, Simonne has also written two more "Fairytales, and she writes "Airspace" for our newsletter, too!

About the Illustrator—Molly Sullivan

Molly received her Bachelor of Fine Arts degree from Ringling School of Art. She is an active member of Seacoast Art Association and a regular exhibitor of her fine art work at the SAA and other galleries.

She is on our staff at Starcrafts LLC, where her special talents in art and art production are significant for the publishing part of our business. Molly will have more art projects ahead!

Molly's eight year old daughter, Reilly, also deserves mention here, since she has served as a prime critic and advisor for this "Planetary Fairytale" project!

A Planetary Fairytale
Acceptance

The first of the fairytales

This charming and beautiful little story tells about the Sun, Moon and each of the planets in our solar system, including two new planets that were added in 2006 after the discovery of Eris and shortly after that, the promotion of Ceres from asteroid to planet. In this story the planets argue whether or not they are willing to accept the two newcomers into their group.

and the fairytale continues....

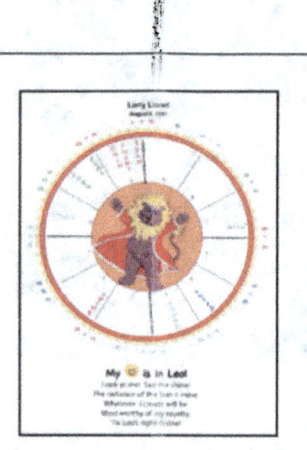

Astro Computing Services
ACS Publications & Starcrafts Publishing
Your best source for everything in astrology!

Easy to Use Software!

Personalized Astrology Lessons

These lessons offer you an opportunity to master the age-old discipline of astrology with your own chart as your primary example. The lessons were designed by Maritha Pottenger to help curious beginners understand all the tools that astrology has to offer. You'll reinforce these lessons with a "homework" assignments that test your knowledge! Have your birth date, time and location ready when you place your order.

32 lessons on one order with notebook—$105.95
Any 6 lessons on one chart—$27.95
One lesson —$6.95   Notebook only— $8.95

The Electronic Astologer Software

The four software packages shown at right are for Windows, XP, Vista or 7. They include the full ACS Atlas database and are very easy to use—no prior knowledge of astrology is needed. You can calculate a horoscope for anyone for whom you have birth date, time and place. Then you can view or print the chart and print a comprehensive text report about it.

"Reveals Your Horoscope" allows you to easily produce and print a natal chart and a text interpretation of it.

"Reveals Your Future " software enables you to produce secondary progressed and transit calculations and print extensive text reports.

"Reveals Your Romance" software allows you to compare any two horocopes, print a rate sheet that rates the partners for attraction, love, sexual sizzle and more. Print extensive interpreted reports.

Each program is $74.95 OR you can buy the "All Three" program for $175.

Other titles by Simonne Joy Murphy

Pluto In Signs, Houses and Aspects

Where is Pluto in Your horoscope?
In this booklet, read about the mythology and astronomy of Pluto, when he was in each of the zodiac signs, and what he means interpretively in each of the houses and in aspect to other planets. Charts of several public figures are shown and interpreted.

$8.95

Ceres In Signs, Houses and Aspects

Eris, a new planet larger than Pluto was discovered in 2006. In response, the International Astronomical union decided to create a new category of "dwarf planet" to include Pluto and Eris. They promoted the largest asteroid Ceres to the new category.

No astrologer has demoted Pluto!

But many astrologers still treat Ceres as just one of the four major asteroids, including her in their charts only when they are also including Juno, Pallas and Vesta.

Why deny Ceres her elevated status?

Here is Ceres in her very own booklet, read about her, get to know her as planet!

$8.95